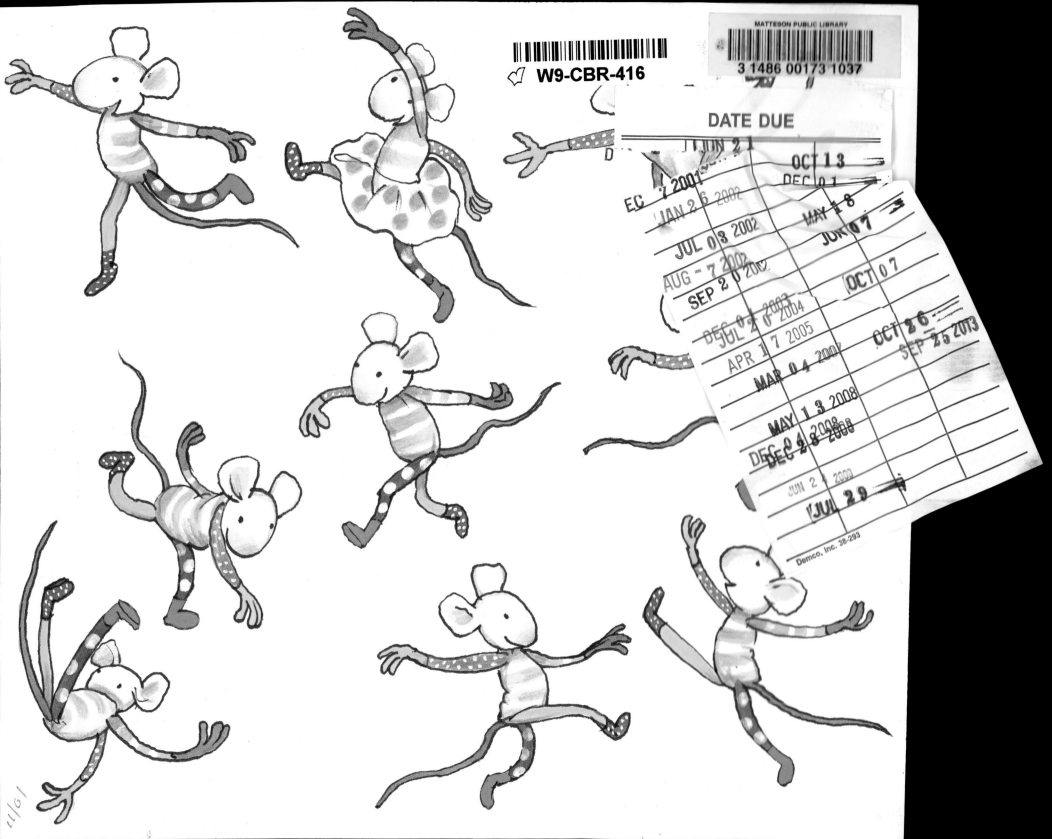

For Ania

Miss Mouse's Day
Copyright © 2001 by Jan Ormerod
Printed in U.S.A. All rights reserved.
www.harperchildrens.com

Library of Congress Cataloging-in-Publication Data
Ormerod, Jan.
Miss Mouse's day / by Jan Ormerod.
p.   cm.
Summary: Miss Mouse's day includes getting dressed, having breakfast, drawing,
having a picnic lunch, gardening, and other activities
before she gets a goodnight kiss and a cuddle.
ISBN 0-688-16333-5 (trade). — ISBN 0-688-16334-3 (le.)
[1. Day—Fiction. 2. Mice—Fiction.] I. Title.
PZ7.0634Mis 2000
[E]—dc21   99-27641

Typography by Hui Hui Su-Kennedy
2 3 4 5 6 7 8 9 10
❖
First Edition

Miss Mouse's Day

That's me!

by Jan Ormerod

HARPERCOLLINSPUBLISHERS

starts with a cuddle,

then a story.

Then I get dressed.

Too hot!

Too big!

Too frilly!

Just right.

For breakfast I like

strawberries   and eggs

and orange juice   and jam.

Time to wash up.

Then I like to draw.

I use pencils

and crayons,

watercolors

and finger paints.

I can't see. . . .

WOW! It's me!

Dressing up is fun.

Too fancy.

Too spooky.

Too scary.

I like lipstick best . . .

and stars, and stripy socks.

I'm gorgeous!

A little lunch.

Then a little exercise.

Whee!   Oops.   HELP!

Saved!

I'm a very fine slider . . .

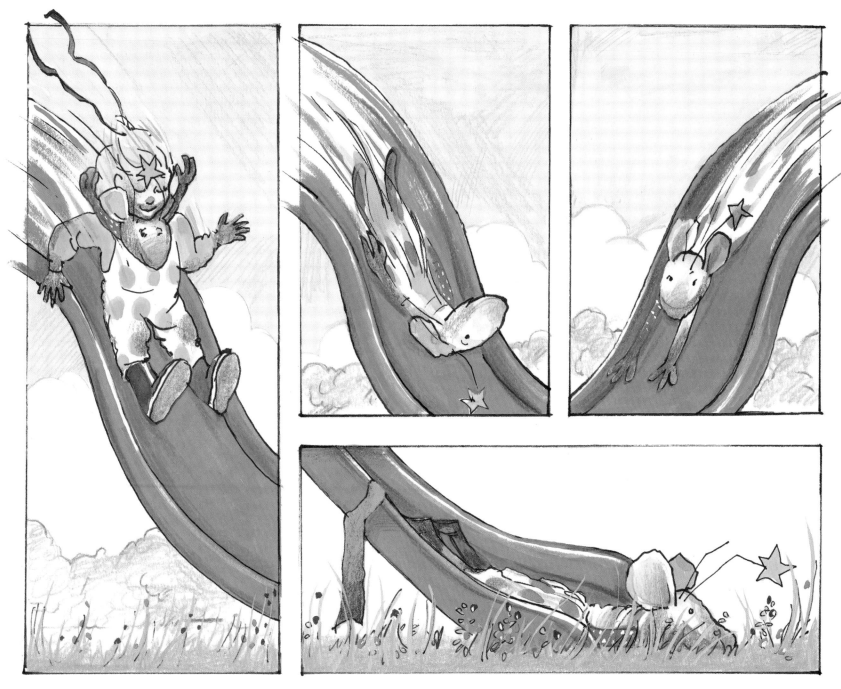

mostly.

I'm a super builder.

Push,

pull,

dig.

A house!

Two houses.

Three houses.

A whole city!

I love flowers  and mud.

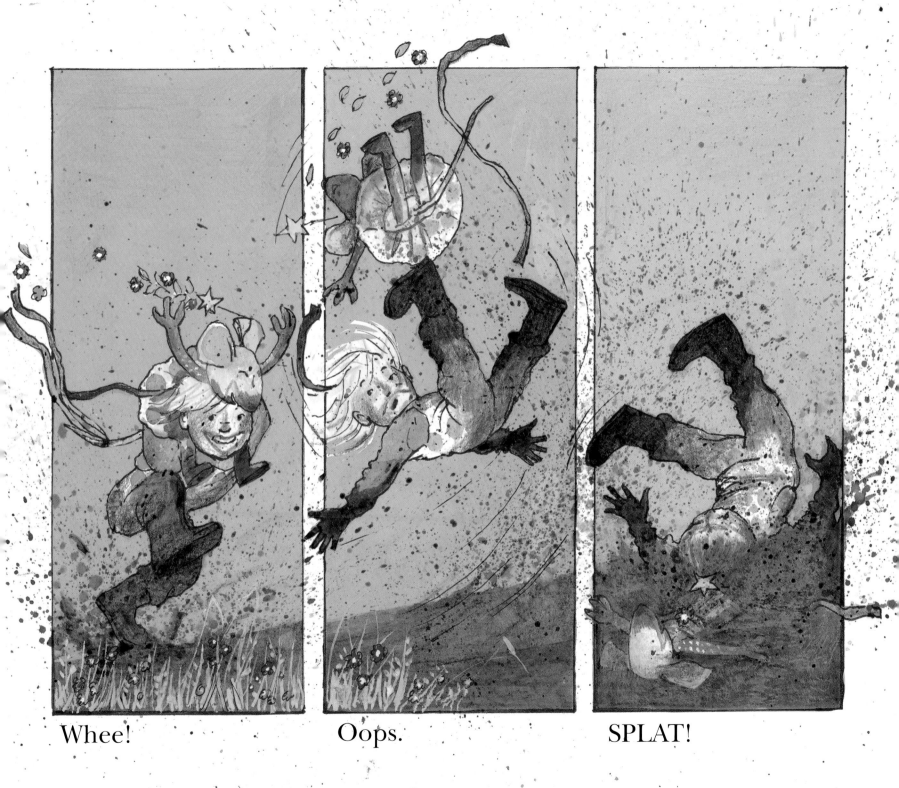

Whee!

Oops.

SPLAT!

"What a mess!

To the tub!"

Oh, dear.   Don't forget me!   Uh-oh . . .

Is that a light?

Whew!

Wash, wring,

towel, spin: clean and dry.

Quiet games

and a story.   A yawn,   then off to bed.

A good night kiss, and my day ends . . .

with a cuddle.

Good night!